SOLDIER BOY

'Did you move them?' asked Martin.
'Why?'

'The finger is curved now.' It was true.

'Yes, I moved them,' Drew said quickly. He shuddered. He wiped the window quickly. He didn't want Martin to realise what he now knew. The finger had written on the window. He had heard it scratching on the glass in the night.

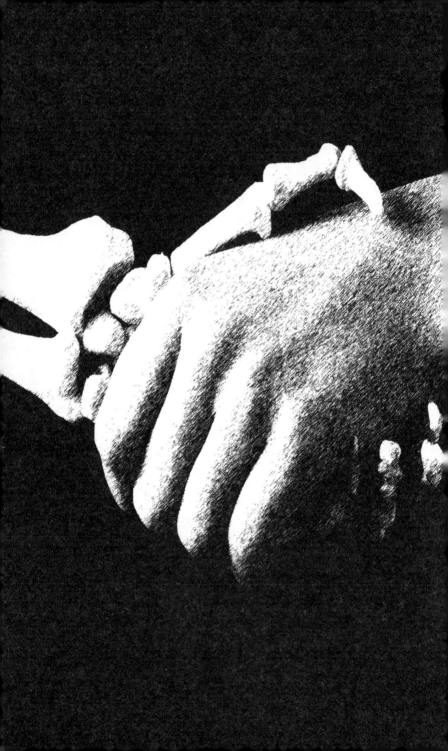

SOLDIER BOY

Titles in the series *On Target*:

SOLDIER BOY

Anne Rooney

READZ●NE

ReadZone Books Limited

50 Godfrey Avenue
Twickenham
TW2 7PF
www.ReadZoneBooks.com

© ReadZone Books Limited 2013

Originally published by Evans Brothers Ltd, London in 2009.

Copyright: © Anne Rooney 2013
The right of Anne Rooney to be identified as the author
of this work has been asserted in accordance with the
Copyright Designs and Patents Act 1988
Design: Nicolet Oost Lievense
Cover design: Jurian Wiese
Images: iStockphoto
Printed by Easy-to-Read Publications

British Library Cataloguing in Publication Data (CIP) is available
for this title.

ISBN 978 1 78322 084 7

Contents

Chapter One

'Drew – look what I've got!'

Martin bounced on to Drew's bed. Drew scowled at him. He hated his little brother rushing into his room without knocking. Drew looked at what Martin held in his hand.

'Cool! A bone. Where did you get it?'

'Outside. I was playing with my lorries. It was in the dirt. Is it from a person?'

'Looks like a bone from a dog's tail,' Drew said. 'Let's clean the mud off.'

They scrubbed the bone under the tap with the nail brush.

'It's definitely a tail bone,' Drew said. But he wasn't sure.

'Let's dig up the rest of the dog,' said Martin.

'OK. Get your wellies.'

They went out into the garden.
Drew grabbed a spade.

'Where was it?' Drew asked.

Martin showed him.

It was a cold, wet day and the mud
was heavy. Drew dug out a big clump.
They broke it up with their fingers.

'Here's another!' cried Martin.

They put it next to the first bone. It
was the same shape, but smaller.
Drew found another bone. It was
bigger. Martin laid them in a row.

'Look, they do make a tail!' he said.

But Drew was quiet. He knew it
wasn't a tail.

Chapter Two

'Let's take them inside,' he said to
Martin.

'Can't we find the whole dog?'

'Not now.'

Drew knew Martin wasn't going to

find a whole dog.

'What sort of dog do you think it is?' asked Martin, following Drew. Drew didn't answer.

'Let's show Mum,' Martin said.

'No. Not yet.'

'Why? Why do you get to choose?' asked Martin.

'Because I'm fifteen and you're six. Because when Mum's at work, I'm in charge. And because she won't let you dig it up in case there are germs.'

They washed the new bones. They laid them in a line again.

'Look,' said Drew. 'What do you notice?'

'They're long,' said Martin. 'Like
a tail.'

Drew spread his hand out next to
the bones.

'Like a finger,' said Drew. 'They're
finger bones. It's shorter than my
finger. It's from a kid.' He bent
his finger. He showed Martin how
it had three bones in it.

Martin gasped.

'Do you think there's a body in
our garden?'

Drew didn't answer. He thought
there was.

'Can we phone the police?' asked
Martin. Martin loved the police. But

Drew didn't want to. The police were trouble.

'Let's dig it up ourselves,' he said. 'Tomorrow's Saturday. We can dig when Mum's at work.'

They put the bones on the window sill, behind the curtain.

Chapter Three

Drew woke with a start. It was the middle of the night. He'd heard a scratching noise. But it stopped. He turned the light on. Everything was the same as before. The curtain moved, just a bit. Then it was still. Maybe there was a mouse. He turned the light off and closed his eyes.

Drew had a paper round on Saturdays. He got up early and dressed in the dark. It was cold outside. He was glad to get home after his round. He ate some cereal and went to his room. Martin had got up, and followed him in.

'Are we going to dig up the body today?' he asked.

Drew pulled back the curtains. There was mist on the window. Spidery letters traced across the mist.

Drew peered at them.

COME AND
FIND ME

Drew turned to Martin.

'Did you do this?'

'Do what?'

Martin couldn't write well yet.
Of course he didn't do it.

'Nothing,' said Drew.

'What does it say? If you don't tell
me, I'll ask Mum.'

Drew raised his hand to wipe it

away. Then he stopped. He picked up his phone and took a picture of it.

'Why did you do that?' asked Martin.

'Evidence,' Drew said.

'Can we dig up the body now?' asked Martin. He reached out for the bones. Drew caught his hand in mid-air.

'Leave them,' he said. 'They're safe here.'

'Did you move them?' asked Martin.

'Why?'

'The finger is curved now.' It was true.

'Yes, I moved them,' Drew said quickly. He shuddered. He wiped the window quickly. He didn't want Martin to realise what he now knew.

The finger had written on the window. He had heard it scratching on the glass in the night.

Chapter Four

Mum went to work at the café at three o'clock. There wasn't much time before it got dark. Drew and Martin went into the garden.

'We'll just use a trowel this time,

said Drew. 'The big spade might break the bones.'

He turned over little clods of earth. They picked through each heavy, grey lump. Sometimes it was hard to tell stones from bones.

By four o'clock, cold rain drizzled on them. Drew stuffed the bones they'd found in his pocket.

'We haven't found any for ages. It's too wet and cold and dark. Let's go inside.'

They washed the bones and arranged them on the floor. It was like doing a jigsaw puzzle.

'We've got most of a hand!' cried

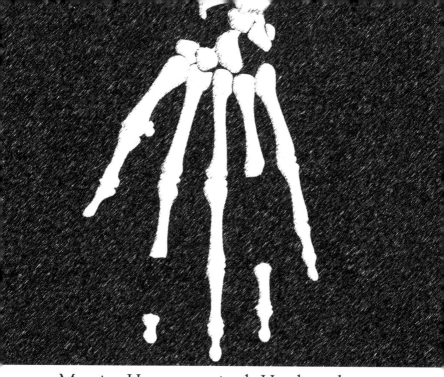

Martin. He was excited. He thought it was just a game. Drew knew it wasn't. Dead people aren't buried in gardens. Not unless they've been murdered. He knew they should tell the police. But he was scared. He'd been cautioned last month. He didn't want any more trouble.

'Why are they all hand bones?' asked Martin. 'Let's find the head!'

He didn't wait for an answer.

'Did the man who lived here before kill someone?' Martin asked.

Drew remembered the man. They had seen him when they moved in last year. He was going to an old people's home. He'd lived here for thirty years. That was long enough to kill someone and bury them in the garden. And for them to rot away.

Drew shivered. But it wasn't from the cold this time.

'Shall we put them on the window sill again?' asked Martin. Drew shook his head. He gathered up the bones and dropped them into a box.

Then he put the lid on. He didn't want them running around in the night again.

Before he went to bed, Drew looked in the box. The bones were still jumbled up. Nothing had happened. But he locked the box in the garden shed, just in case.

Chapter Five

The next morning, Martin came in holding the bones.

'Can we dig up the body now?'

'Where did you get those?' Drew asked.

'From the bathroom,' said Martin.
Drew swallowed. How could they
have been in the bathroom? He'd
locked them in the shed.

He grabbed Martin's wrist.

'How did you get the bones,
Martin?' he asked again.

Martin's lip wobbled. He was
going to cry.

'They really were in the bathroom.
You left them by the tap. Didn't you?'

Drew didn't answer. He didn't
want to dig up any more bones now.
He wished they'd never dug up any
at all. He wanted to put them back
and forget about it.

'You're hurting me,' whined Martin. Drew let go.

'Can we go and dig now?' asked Martin. 'I want to dig. You said we could.'

'No. Shhhh. Don't let Mum hear. What do you think she'd do if she thought there was a body in the garden?'

Martin shrugged.

'She might help dig it up?'

'No, she'd go to the police. Then you wouldn't have any fun.'

'I would! There'd be police cars, and policemen. And dogs! I love dogs!'

'No,' Drew said firmly. 'There's

probably nothing there. Mum goes to work at eleven. We'll look then.'

They worked with the trowel in the heavy soil. Drew tried not to find anything. Every few seconds, Martin shouted, 'Here's one!' but it never was. It was a stone, or a stick.

Once it was a small metal ball, very rusty.

'Can I keep that ball?' Martin asked. Drew handed it to him. It wasn't interesting.

In the afternoon, it started snowing.

'I'm bored,' whined Martin. 'It's too cold. I'm going inside.'

Drew followed him. They hadn't found a body. Or even any bones. Drew was relieved.

Chapter Six

'No school!' yelled Martin, rushing into Drew's room. 'Snow day!'

Drew went to the window. He pulled back the curtains. It was true. The world was covered in thick white snow.

No, not everywhere was white. There were bare patches. One in the garden. And lots in the field next door. They were odd shapes. They reminded Drew of something. He couldn't think what. And then he knew. Body outlines – the body outlines drawn at crime scenes. He pulled the curtains shut quickly before Martin noticed.

'Go and get dressed, Martin,' he said. Martin stared at him.

'Why? I don't have to go to school.'

'So you can play in the snow, stupid.'

Martin ran off. Drew opened the curtains again. They were definitely body outlines. The one in the garden was quite near where they'd been digging, where they found the hand. But they had dug and dug and found nothing. Drew thought of something. He grabbed his phone and took photos of the body outlines. When the snow melted, they wouldn't know where they had been. But why were there so many? How many people had the old man killed?

Chapter Seven

They went out into the garden. Drew glanced at the field. The snow looked patchy. You couldn't see the shapes. You had to see them from above. Was that why no one had seen them before? Or weren't they there before? Maybe it was because he had taken the bones.

They went to where they'd been digging. It was covered in snow. Drew bit his lip and thought. This wasn't right. If there was a body there, why wasn't the snow melted in an outline, like the other places? But why was it melted at all? They were just bones. It shouldn't be melted. Drew shuddered.

Martin started making a snowman.

'Help me,' he called to Drew. 'You make the body, I'll make the head.'

Martin was rolling a snowball over the ground.

'Stop!' shouted Drew. Martin was rolling towards the outline. He'd spoil it.

'But I want to make a snowman. Please help.'

Drew sighed. Martin would get cold and go inside. Drew could investigate then. He laid his trowel down inside the body outline so he'd know where it was. Then he helped Martin make a snowman.

Soon, Martin went inside to play.

Drew was scared, but he wanted to know what was going on. He thought he'd dig just a bit. The ground was frozen solid. It took a long time to dig even a small way down. But then he hit something hard. Hard, like bone. He'd found it. He'd found the body.

The snow was stinging his face. His fingers ached with cold. He uncovered a leg – one long bone, a knee cap, two shorter bones. This would take forever. He had to go in – he couldn't leave Martin alone any longer. But he couldn't leave half a body uncovered in the garden.

He pulled a wheelbarrow from behind the shed and turned it upside down over the bones. Mum wouldn't use the wheelbarrow in the snow.

Chapter Eight

Next day, the snow was melting.
There were big patches everywhere.
Drew couldn't make out the body
shapes any more. He was glad he
had a photo.

When Drew got home from school, there was a police car outside the house. The blue light was flashing. Striped tape circled the garden. It said 'Crime scene' again and again. Drew's mother was waiting by the door. She didn't look pleased. Uh-oh.

'There's a body – a skeleton – in the garden. Why didn't you tell me? You can't just dig it up yourself! What were you thinking of? Someone has been killed, and buried in our garden. Don't you understand how serious that is?'

'How did you find out?' he asked lamely.

'How did I find out? There are leg bones under the wheelbarrow! Do you think I'm stupid?'

'I didn't think you'd look.'

Drew's mother sighed.

'Just go inside.'

A police officer asked Drew questions about how he found the bones. Drew didn't tell him about the hand. He told them Martin found the leg when he was playing.

'Was someone murdered?' Drew asked.

'Not recently,' the policeman said. 'It takes years for a body to rot away.'

Just then, another policeman came in. He held something wrapped in a plastic bag.

'No need to worry about this one Gavin. Look.' He showed them what he held. It was a very old gun.

'It's a musket, mate. Comes from the Civil War. It's a nice one. One of my hobbies, old guns. We'll have to take this to forensics.

'That chap's been lying in your garden for 350 years. We've got most of him now. We're just missing a rib. You haven't found one, have you?' he asked Drew.

Drew shook his head. He was puzzled. Weren't they going to ask about the hand?

'Is that all that's missing?' he asked.

'Yep. Pretty good, eh? He's been

undisturbed all that time. Must have been the floods in the autumn brought the bones up to the surface.'

Chapter Nine

Martin was in the bathroom looking at the box of bones.

'Why didn't they want his hand?' he asked Drew.

'It wasn't his,' Drew said. 'Not

unless he had three.'

'So whose is it?'

'I don't know.'

Drew laid the bones out to make a hand shape again. He laid his own hand over the top.

'Just a kid,' he mused, 'smaller than me. Imagine that, being a soldier as a boy.'

Martin shuddered.

'That's spooky,' he said.

Drew let out a horrific scream. Martin jumped.

'What is it?' he whimpered.

Drew was shaking his hand violently. He didn't even look at

Martin. They both looked at Drew's hand. The bone hand had moved. The bone fingers slotted between Drew's fingers. It was holding his hand.

However much he shook it, it didn't come off. He smashed his hand against the side of the bath. The bones fell on the floor in a pile. A trickle of blood ran down the back of Drew's hand.

Drew's face was as white as the bones.

'We have to get rid of it,' he whispered. 'Let's put it back.' But he knew he couldn't pick it up. How could they put it back? They didn't dare touch it.

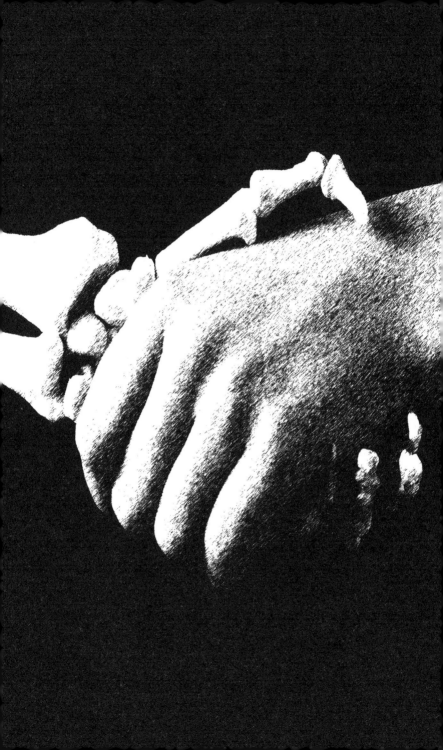

'I'll get the dustpan,' Drew said.
'We can sweep them up.'

He moved towards the door.
Martin clung to his legs, crying.

'Don't leave me with it!' he yelled.

'Come with me, then.'

When they came back the bones
hadn't moved. Drew held his breath.

He swept them quickly into the
dustpan. Nothing happened. They
were just bones.

'Open the window, Martin.'

Martin just sat on the floor.

'Do it!'

'I can't! I can't do the catch!' he
sobbed.

Drew put the dustpan down and opened the window. He tried to keep his eyes on the bones. Then he flung the bones out into the garden and slammed the window.

'There! All gone!' and he hugged him so tightly Martin couldn't breathe.

Chapter Ten

It was dark. The numbers on his clock glowed: 3:20. Drew listened to the scratching noise. His blood ran cold. He knew what it was. He didn't dare turn the light on. The noise stopped. He lifted the curtain. It was very dark. There was frost on the window already. Then it started. Tap, tap. Bone glinted white through the glass, tapping on the window. Tap, tap, tap. One finger was stretched out, the others curled into a hand. Tap, tap, tap. Drew closed his eyes. It must be a dream, a bad dream. It must be. Tap, tap, tap, tap. He clamped the pillow over his head. Tap, tap, tap, tap. Then silence. Drew lay in the dark for hours, too afraid to move.

It was still dark when Drew got up at seven o'clock. He was scared to

pull the curtains back – but he knew
he had to. He counted to three. He
ripped them back sharply before he
lost his nerve.

'*Bury it – soldier boy.*'

The letters were scratched into
the ice outside the window. He
couldn't wipe them away.

Drew gasped and closed the
curtain.

'What does it say?'

Martin was in the doorway,
watching him.

'It says "Bury it",' Drew said. There
was no point lying. Martin had seen
it. He would only tell Mum.

'Bury who?'

'The soldier boy's hand,' Drew answered.

'Do we have to? I'm scared.'

He clutched Drew's pyjamas.

'Me too. But I think we do have to. Or it will come back.'

'Can we tell Mum?' Martin asked.

'Best not. We're in trouble already.'

'But I'm scared.'

'Let's get on with it,' said Drew. He tried to sound brave. He would feel brave if he sounded brave. But how on earth would they find the dead boy?

Of course! His phone! He'd taken a picture of the outlines! Drew turned the computer on. He copied the photos on to the computer. He zoomed in on the picture. It filled the screen.

'Find a small one,' he said to Martin.

'There!' Martin jabbed at the screen. He was right. Near the hedge, in the field. Drew clicked on print.

'OK, let's go. Quick, before Mum gets up.'

Chapter Eleven

They took the spade and the printout and climbed the gate into the field. It was just getting light. They found the place where the small outline had been. The ground was very hard. Digging it hurt Drew's hands.

'Stop!' shouted Martin. 'There's something pale.'

Drew bent down. He brushed the earth away with his fingers. Bone. Smooth, hard bone.

'Let's get the hand,' Drew said. He'd left the bones lying on the grass under the window. He hadn't wanted to touch them. But there was no choice. They had to put the hand with the body. They went back to the garden together. There were the bones, under the window. They weren't in a pile.

They made a pattern. No, words.

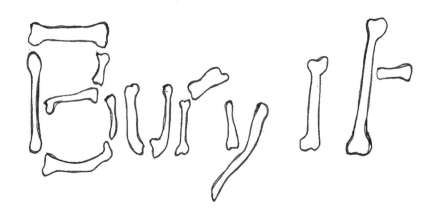

Bury it

Nervously, Drew poked a bone.
Nothing happened. He picked one
up. He put it in his coat pocket.
He split the rest between two
pockets. They couldn't do anything
in separate pockets, surely?

Drew dug a hole near the bone
they'd dug up. He tipped in the
bones.

'Do it nicely,' said Martin. 'Make is straight.'

Drew was about to refuse. But what if the hand came back? He made the hole bigger. Then he laid the bones out in the right shape. He held his breath. Nothing happened.

As quickly as he could, he covered the bones with earth. Then he stamped it flat. *Stay in there*, he thought.

As they walked back to the house, it started to snow. It snowed and snowed. Drew watched the snow fall from his bedroom window. The snow covered the garden and the field completely. There were no bare patches. He breathed a sigh of relief.

They'd done it – and the soldier boy was gone.

Titles in the series On Target

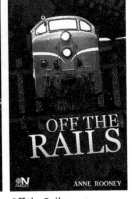